Almost nothing, yet Everything

A book about Water

Written by
Hiroshi Osada

Illustrated by
Ryōji Arai

Translated from the Japanese by
David Boyd

Enchanted Lion Books
NEW YORK

It shines brighter than anything.

It runs clearer than anything.

It has no color,

but can be any color.

It has no shape,

but can take any shape.

You can touch it, but you can't hold it.

Even if you slice into it, it won't be cut.

It can slip through your fingers, like it's nothing at all.

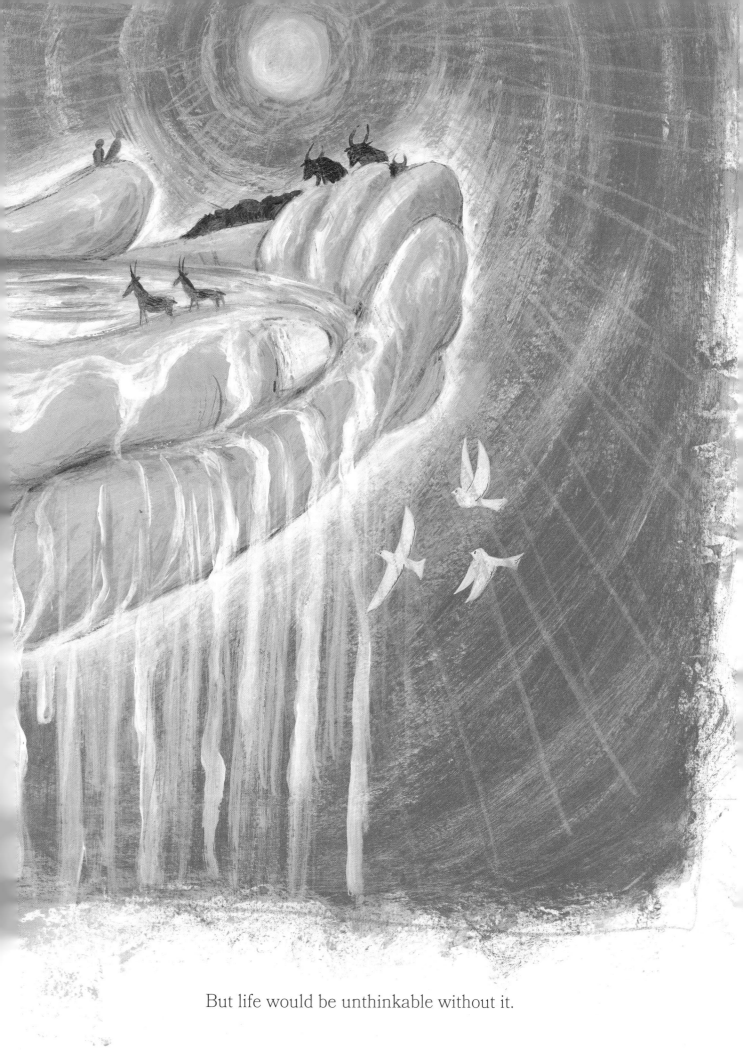

But life would be unthinkable without it.

You can find almost anything inside it.

Even when nothing is there.

Take a look—there you are, with the sky behind you.

It flows like tears.

It rains down like falling stars.

It cascades and courses.

It fills and overflows.

Only oxygen and hydrogen, simple as can be.

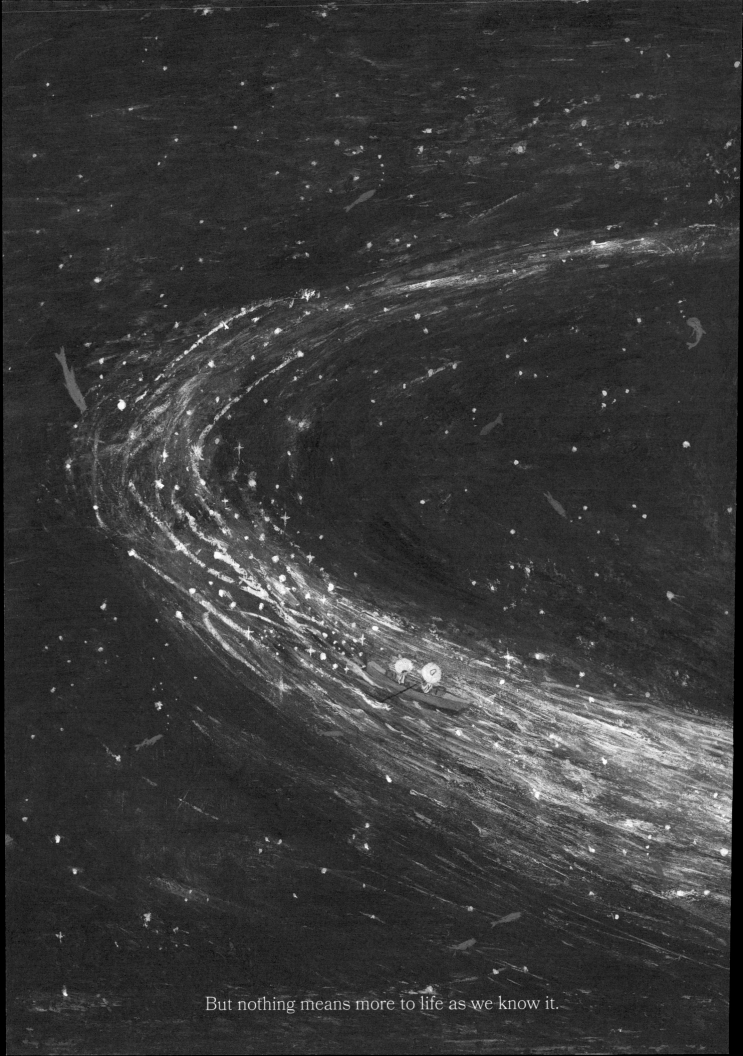

But nothing means more to life as we know it.

Like the mother of us all, it creates life.

Like blood, it courses through us, refreshing our spirits.

It is the pee of life.

Then the child asks: Is it the pee-pee of the gods?
It sure is, I answer.

And then, I wrote this poem.

Hiroshi Osada was born in Fukushima City in 1939. He graduated from Waseda University in 1963. Two years later, he debuted as a poet with *This Journey*. In 1982, he received the Mainichi Publishing Culture Award for *The Bookstore of the Century*. In 1991, he won the Robō-no-ishi Literary Prize. In 1998, Osada was awarded the first Kuwabara Takeo Prize for *The Making of Memories*. In 2000, his collaboration with Ryōji Arai, *A Forest Picture Book*, earned the Kōdansha Publishing Culture Award for Children's Literature. His second collaboration with Ryōji Arai, *Every Color of Light*, followed. He died in 2015.

Ryōji Arai was born in Yamagata Prefecture in 1956. He studied art at Nihon University. In 1990, he published his first picture book, *Melody*. In 1997, he won the Shōgakukan Children's Publishing Culture Prize for *The Lying Moon*. In 1999, Arai's *Journey of Riddles* received the Special Award at the Bologna Book Fair. He won the Astrid Lindgren Memorial Award, the highest international award in children's literature, in 2005. In 2009, he won the JBBY Prize for *The Sun Organ*. In 2012, *It's Morning — Let's Open A Window* received the Sankei Children's Book Award.

David Boyd is Assistant Professor of Japanese at the University of North Carolina at Charlotte. His translations have appeared in *Monkey Business International, Granta*, and *Words Without Borders*, among other publications.

www.enchantedlion.com

First English language edition published in 2021 by Enchanted Lion Books
248 Creamer Street, Studio 4. Brooklyn, NY 11231

English-language translation copyright © 2021 by Enchanted Lion Books
English-language edition copyright © 2021 by Enchanted Lion Books

Mizu no Ehon © 2019 Atsushi Osada, Takashi Osada / Ryōji Arai.
All rights reserved. First published in Japan in 2019 by Kodansha Ltd., Tokyo.
Publication rights for this English edition arranged through Kodansha Ltd., Tokyo.

Book design by Eugenia Mello.

All rights reserved under International and Pan-American Copyright Conventions
A CIP record is on file with the Library of Congress
ISBN 978-1-59270-357-9

Printed in 2021 by Grafiche AZ, Verona | First Printing